The Inappropriate Library
by
Kim Isaac Greenblatt

Shockingly Awesome Press
Published In West Hills, California

The Inappropriate Library
by Kim Isaac Greenblatt

Published by Shockingly Awesome Press in West Hills, California, USA.

ISBN-13 978-0-9777282-8-2

LCCN# 2007910324
January 2008

Dedicated to Jacob and Arianna!

TABLE OF CONTENTS

Billy North

"Text me?" Jake asked.

"Sure," I said. "As long as I can get a signal from our new place."

"Oh, man. You should be able to get a cell phone signal or Internet from anywhere, man."

I got into the car with Mom and my sister, Veronika. I waved good-bye to Jake till I could no longer see him in the distance.

"You'll make new friends when you get to New Alexandria, honey", Mom said.

"I guess."

I had no idea at the time that the friends I would make would be talking books.

Talking books like the Fun Facts of the Ancient World 1102AD Edition...

Excerpt From Fun Facts of the Ancient World 1102 AD Edition

Greetings, peace and joy upon you, my trusted friend. If you are reading this, indeed, you can be trusted. After all, the library has survived for better or worse, because of trust. We, who are trying to find a cosmic balance, rely on trust as well.

This may look like a lot of boring text but I can promise you that it is anything BUT boring.

First, we need to set records straight.

It is indeed true that the Library (with a capital "L" from now on, if you will graciously indulge me) existed before Alexander's time; its true nature became apparent during that period of The First Enlightenment. Though accounts state that the Library was established around 3 B.C., the truth is that it existed before that in some shape or form that was not commonly known by many except those initiated in schools of the Mysteries.

It should make sense to you, trusted friend, because if we are to first surmise that if in the Beginning, there was the Word, would it not make sense that somewhere, sometime, the Word would be written down?

What do you suppose would happen if somebody had the power with one word to create whatever he or she wanted?

"I want to control the weather!"

"I want all the gold in the world."

How about if whatever they said destroyed what ever they wanted? You wonder where the origins of magical "spells" came from?

"I want my enemies dead!"

Ahhh! I can see the light flickering in your eyes indicating enlightenment.

Yes, that is it exactly.

Somewhere between the birth of Creation and now, the first sounds, the first Word, if you will was captured and saved.

Unlike recording devices of today, the best we could clumsily do was either recite to one another the sound or write down what we thought was the sound and pass it down for others to experiment with.

Results though at times seemingly miraculous or catastrophic, were still far from being what a supreme deity would be able to do. Perhaps that is for the best, eh?

Human nature, being what it is, decided to take the Word and use it at times in what we shall call not-so-beneficial ways.

There were the wars. Beings of incomparable power yet evenly matched fighting for years causing damage to cities, killing millions, and polluting the environment. The sides were too evenly matched. Within these factions, cooler heads prevailed and decided to come to a compromise.

So with the early wars, the wise men of the day decided to collect all the documents, scrolls, parchment and early books that had the approximation of these powerful words and collect them somewhere safe where they all could watch over these powerful men.

Men and women come and go and with them their hopes and dreams. Some of the caretakers were less than dutiful in their care and started using the Library to develop powers to control nations.

Unlike the overt battles, they tried doing this in subtle ways getting leaders to do their bidding through guile and corruption. Other of the Library's caretakers seeing this used what they could of the Library to fight back.

I am a part of the group that fought back.

Sadly, the majority of our group came to the conclusion that the Library must cease to exist in order for mankind, even life on the planet to have a decent shot at continuing. We cried to the Heavens.

"Save us! Do something!"

The universe or whatever you want to call it decided to listen and try to remedy this error by wiping out the Library. The first attempt was with water.

Lots of water.

In fact, throughout all world cultures you will read of this water.

The Great Flood that happened was more for the benefit of ruining all documentation in the Library then the universe-cleaning house. Granted, it was an easy two-for-the price-of-one deal and it sobered up humanity for several hundred years at least. The shame was that it also resulted in a great deal of beneficial information being lost.

I've debated with others that if we ultimately lose the Library, a great deal of aid to humanity and its evolution may be gone forever. Another sad item was that the Library learned from its mistake.

Fun Fact #1-The Library cannot be destroyed with water anymore.

Since then, the Heavens seem to have thrown their hands up in resignation as well since any prayers seem to have fallen on deaf ears! Perhaps it was by our doing and powers that the waters covered the earth and not some deity. That would indeed be sad!

Fast-forward to about 250 BC and we have the reign of Ptolemy II from Egypt. He built this as a supplement to his father's contribution, the temple of the Muses.

What history texts fail to tell you is that the temple of the Muses had taught hundreds of people as best as they could the basis of the Word.

Some of the people literally became what they believed.

Crazy, dear reader? Is it any crazier than what people can do in this day and age?

Do not people who are under the influence of alcohol, narcotics or hypnosis think they can be animals, feelings, and creatures? I see you nodding your head so I will not belabor the point..

Of course without devices to record what they would sound like, the followers had their disciples write books and cast their sounds through letters into books!

Incredible is it not? The power of the Library was amazing.

What was more incredible was that a lot of these people had hoped to become immortal and control all life. Human nature did not evolve or change as some of these beings gained power.

It only corrupted them faster.

Sadly, that left others the horrible choice of either letting future generations die or willingly accept a bizarre form of immortality themselves to bond in text to guard against these beings from ever attaining their goal.

That was the purpose of the supplemental library. Disciples of those of us who believed the corruption must be kept in check; we transferred ourselves into the texts themselves to stay in the library. Together with the texts saved from the temple of the Muses, the Library, as we know it today was formed.

The Library has been known to be sneaky.

Back in the day, it was mandatory that whenever a book came into Alexandria, it was confiscated and copied in the Library. It was thought to be that all world knowledge should be stored and copied in the Library. Ha! The Library was waiting to see how it could extend its reach into the world.

Would the people of the day wonder how quickly that their book was copied! A lot of times, their book might be replaced with a book from the Library that would go on to alter the lives of kings and commoners alike! The book would go out and guide its owner to greatness - or madness - depending on the nature of the book.

We would sometimes be able to get out ourselves and stop the evil books from corrupting civilization.

Fun Fact #2-Not all books from the Library are bad to read. The problem is that sometimes it gets to be hard to tell the difference.

It came to a point where the Library was making a concerted effort to go out completely after some wars to spread itself throughout the world and make civilization in the image that it wanted. A lot of people think that it was Caesar, Aurelian, the decree of Theophilus or the Muslim conquest that destroyed the Library.

Kindly let me set the record straight.

None of them destroyed the Library. We destroyed it ourselves with fire. Any other fires attributed to anybody else were insignificant. That leads us to our next Fun Fact!

Fun Fact #3-The Library cannot be destroyed with fire anymore.

Good luck and please go to the next chapter for more Fun Facts and information!

Oh, before I go, please do not forget this important fun fact:

Fun Fact #4 - The Library has a wicked sense of humor. For example, do not trust librarians named Ptolemy! They are nothing like the true Ptolemy was.

-from the Fun Facts of the Ancient World 1102 AD Edition

Billy North

I didn't have much say in the decision to move to New Alexandria. It was Mom's decision and Veronika (yeah, she is pretentious and spells her name now with a "k", I know, I know), and I went along with it. My mom wanted to move out of L.A. while she had some equity in the house that Dad left us and she said she was sick and tired of the rat race.

I was kind of pissed off but she said I could still play X-Box Live with my friends.   I mean, they can still visit me and stuff but we could still talk with headsets so it is still cool.

Kinda.

New Alexandria, California is just north of Santa Barbara. We drove up in about half a day and the weather was pretty good for California winter.

We had winds going 80 miles an hour and the U-Haul truck we were in only swerved towards the railing once while we were on PCH. I almost peed my pants when that happened.

Mom, Veronika and I were all huddled together in the truck's cab. When the gust hit we slid sideways about two feet onto oncoming traffic and an angry looking older man and his wife driving a Lexus nearly hit us. They braked just in time and looked just as scared as we probably did.

Mom paid some local guys to help haul our stuff into our new house. The new house was about the size of our old one, a four bedroom one level house and we had a larger yard then back in Los Angeles. Mom had gotten a job with the city of Alexandria as a city accountant and said that she would make as much as she would staying in Los Angeles.

We started school in January, which wasn't too bad and we had half a year left before summer. I was going to turn 14 in March and eighth grade was pretty much eighth grade as far as I was concerned. As long as I could play my video games and skate I was cool.

I met the neighbors, the Mendozas right away. They were an older couple and they had a daughter, Tricia. She was my age and in a couple of my classes. What was really weird was that none of the kids had cell phones, ipods or any computers at home.

Books. Lots and lots of books.

After school one day, I just asked Tricia about it.

"Tricia, what's the deal with all these books?"

She took me to the library.

The City of New Alexandria Library was located in the heart of town next to the City Hall and across the street from the fire and police departments. The building was made of brick and looked like it had been around for a long time. I walked to the library with Tricia since it wasn't too far away from our houses. The air was cool later in the day and the sun was starting to set. There were a lot of other kids and grown ups walking in and out of the library. Tricia is a little taller than me and was wearing a black jacket to match her long black hair and black tights. She was wearing short black boots. I liked her.

She was hot.

I was trying to play it cool with her and a cool thing about moving to a new town was that she would get to know me for me now and not as somebody who had done something stupid in the second grade.

Points scored for you, Mom.

We walked into the Library. The doors looked like they had some scripture on them that looked like it was some ancient language. For all I know it could have been some calligraphy of some English words but it sure looked older to me. I walked inside. Footsteps made a clackety-clackety sound over a grill on the floor as we approached the main room.

There was a rotunda in the center of a big hallway. All around the rotunda were shelves of books. Children and adults were all over the library reading.

"Ah, can I help you?" asked a tall, thin man from behind the rotunda.

"Mr. Ptolemy, this is Billy North. He just moved to town and he needs a library card."

"Okay, Tricia. Nice to meet you, Mr. North." he extended his hand.

I reached over to shake it. It was like shaking hands with electricity or something. You know that feeling you get when you walk on a shag rug in your socks and go and try and shock your sister? It was a lot like that only weirder. When he let go the tingling continued in my hand for about another minute.

"Quite a handshake you have there, Mr. North."

"Uh, whatever and call me Billy."

He pulled out a library card application from seemingly nowhere and handed it to me with a pen.

"Just fill out the information and I can issue you a temporary card until one of your parents signs the form and you bring it back to me."

"Uh, okay."

It took about two minutes to fill out the application. Mr. Ptolemy seemed to be talking to himself as he typed the information into a computer terminal. He printed out a paper library card with my name on it. He handed me back the application.

"Make sure your mom or dad signs this. Bring it back to me tomorrow."

"Yes sir."

The way he said it sounded more like a command and I was scared if I didn't do it something would happen to me.
I took the application and folded it in my pocket. Where did Tricia go?

Tricia was walking over to a series of shelves. As I started to walk towards her I was knocked down onto my butt. I looked up and saw a big beefy blonde haired kid.

"Hey jerk, you got in Big Jim's way. Aren't ya gonna say, sorry?"

"Uh, sorry?"

Big Jim was wearing a lumberjack shirt and jeans and clodhopper boots. He was bigger than me. I made it back to my feet and looked at the idiot. The last thing I wanted was getting into a fight with some local yahoo and starting some vendetta.

"That wasn't good enough."

I looked at Big Jim and he looked like he was a total loser. Mr. Ptolemy had appeared quickly next to Big Jim. I didn't even see how he moved next to him that quickly!

"Leave him alone, Mr. Andrews. This is a library and not a schoolyard."

"Yes sir, Mr. Ptolemy."

Big Jim made a motion with two fingers towards me and then towards his eyes. He was so stupid he did the "I am keeping my eyes on you" hand motions backwards. What a stink hole. I didn't think there would be enough books in this library to smarten this guy up.

Tricia came back over to me. "Big Jim is an idiot. He has issues. Don't let him get to you."

"I don't want him anywhere near me if that is okay with you."

Tricia laughed. Man, she is so cute.

We walked over to the Non-Fiction shelves and started walking down the aisle.

"See if there is a book that calls to you."

"Huh?"

"You know, see if there is a book that you might like or if a book likes you!" she giggled.

"What is your favorite book?"

She walked over to a shelf and pulled out a book. It looked like it was written back when dinosaurs ruled the earth. The cover was ratty and dark blue and it was hard to make out the letters. They were faded gold and they read "I Love Verbs".

"You are kidding me, right?"

"No, this is my absolute favorite in the whole world."

"Okay, okay that's cool."

"You think I am strange don't you?"

"Yeah, actually."

"Well, the book just called to me and you know what, it was just the book I needed!"

"I don't know if I could find a book that would call to me like that."

"Don't be too sure," she smirked.

As I started to walk down the aisles I started to think that she was cute but weird when I felt it. It was a tugging in my gut. The tugging spread to my chest, up my neck and into my forehead. I just started walking towards books down an aisle. I stopped and I felt the urge to pull out a book. As I started to look down the shelf, I started walking to another row.

Tricia was quietly keeping up with me, "Looks like you are having a bunch of books call out to you."

What was weird was that none of the other kids or adults in the library seemed to care that I was moving around aisle-to-aisle at a pretty decent pace. It was like I had to find the right book for me!

I approached another couple of shelves but at the last minute the tugging feelings drew me to another aisle. I saw on the corner that the section read "Non Fiction" and I walked over to a shelf. I looked down and had this feeling like I was going to meet an old friend. I picked up my book.

The book that called to me.

It was a gray covered book with pictures of Japan, Egypt, Rome, Paris, London and Washington DC on the cover. The pictures were faded and they wrapped around the book. The letters on the spine were faded but the title of the book was clear on the cover -The Burger International Architecture Guide 1947 Edition.

I looked at this book and it was like something had been missing from my life and I had found it. I can't explain it any better than that. Despite the fact that it looked like a piece of trash, this book was something I had wanted my whole life and didn't even know it.

"You were right, Tricia."

"I know," she smiled.

She walked closer and gave me a kiss on the cheek!

Mr. Ptolemy

Mr. Ptolemy was upset because he was hoping that one of the other books would have successfully called out to Billy North. Additionally, he was aggravated because despite his best efforts he could not upload any of the library books onto the Internet (again!). Looming over him was the fear that he might lose. Control over the Library might slip away from him.

He tracked down Big Jim.

"Jim?"

"Yes sir?"

"Can you do me a favor and keep an eye out and watch that new boy Billy North for me?"

"I don't like him, sir. I still haven't found a book that calls out to me, either."

"I have a special book I have been saving for you, Jim."

Jim's eyes lit up.

Mr. Ptolemy led Jim to an aisle in the back of the library.

Jim's eyes widened. "You mean I get to check out one of the books from the reference section?"

Mr. Ptolemy smiled. "Yep. And I think you will like this one. Just be careful with it."

It was a book with tanks, aircraft and military ships. It was Mabel's Books of Weapons 1976.

Billy North

Can life get any better? She kissed me!
Man!

I waited till we were out of the library and
gave her a hug and kiss on her cheek. She
returned my hug with a gentle squeeze and
blushed a little. The street lamps were
coming on as we started walking towards
our homes.

"Hey, can I instant message you later, or do
you have a cell phone I can text?"

She smiled. "I don't have a cell phone."

"What do you do when your Mom or Dad
want to reach you?"

"I tell them what I am planning on doing for
the day and they trust me."

Trust, what a concept! I held the library
book in one hand and extended my other

hand towards Tricia's. She grabbed my fingers. "Your hand is so warm, Billy."

"Let me warm yours up." I was sounding like a total dork but I didn't care. She actually kissed me! And I kissed her! Man!

"Billy, I need to do some reading tonight and you probably will want to get to reading your book as well."

"Huh? Oh yeah, the book." I looked back at the book and remembered the feeling of finding an old friend rush back into me. I held Tricia's hand as we continued walking through the streets. Car headlights flashed in between the streetlights. We could see the houses down the block with their lights on. They reminded me of Christmas luminaries with candles inside of them. At least it felt like it was Christmas inside of me.

I could feel Tricia's hand warming up. We slowed down and stopped in front of her house. We could see her Mom and Dad sitting down at the dining room table. "I like you, Billy."

"I like you to, Tricia." I leaned forward to kiss her on the cheek and she blocked it with a hand.

"Not here! I don't want to get teased by my Mom or Dad!"

"Okay, okay." Total buzz kill city...

I walked up the driveway to my house.

"Hey, Justin Timberlake, what happened?"

Great. Veronika. "Nothing happened, I just was walking home with her."

"I could see that. She stopped you ice cold, boy! But keep at it. Be crafty, be crafty."

"You suck, Veronika."

"Too bad she won't", Veronika laughed as we both went into the house.

I could smell the turkey that Mom had reheated from the hallway. I placed the book down on the table near the front door. After hanging up our jackets we went into the dining room. The turkey was on the table. Mom had entered from the kitchen wearing her purple sweater that she liked to say would "highlight her assets".

"Going out tonight, Mom?"

"The sweater was a give-away, Billy? Sinclair from work asked me out. His wife passed away about the same time dad did. Go wash your hands."

Veronika and I marched into the bathroom. Veronika yelled, "Is he hot?"

"I don't know about hot but he's cute."

We washed our hands and then toweled them dry quickly. I could smell the garlic mashed potatoes and beans that were on the table. We walked back into the dining room.

Mom sat down as we did and started serving us. I took a pitcher of apple juice and poured a glass for Veronika, Mom and myself.

"We're going to a movie and then coffee. I won't be out too late because it is a work night."

"Can I go out on dates on school nights?" Veronika asked as she took a bite of turkey.

"No. This is a case of do as I say, not as I do."

"Some great example you're setting, Mom", I chimed in. The food was great. I was happy that Mom looked so happy. She must really be into this guy. I hope he isn't a jerk.

"Time for Mom to change the subject. So what did you guys do today?"

"Went to the library after school," Veronika said.

"What? Me too." I wondered if Veronika even knew how to read sometimes.

"There was this cute guy I am trying to crush on. He likes to go to the library so I figured I would go too."

I hated to think that my sister thought the way that I did but I guess great minds think alike. Or my great mind and her dufus one.

"Oh? That's nice. How about you, Billy?"

"I ended up at the library as well. It looks like there isn't much to do in this town and the kids never seem to have heard about the Internet."

Mom tossed her hair back. "That's a funny thing. From what I hear at work, the city has been trying for years to get good Internet reception through cable, wireless or DSL. They are trying something called FIOS as well but there are always line troubles. For some reason, this town cannot connect to the internet. We can get some email but it is text only at work. Weird and tough to get use to."

"But console games work?"

"Yeah, your game systems can connect just fine but there is no web connected playing. Computer and cell service is real spotty here."

"Billy has the hots for Tricia," Veronika said matter-of-factly without missing a piece of food going into her mouth.

Pig.

"Mom, I can explain. I just like her. We ended up going to the library together and she likes me."

Mom reached over and stroked my head. "That's wonderful, dear! Just don't let her get in the way of your studies and don't get her pregnant."

"Mom!?" Veronika and I screamed at once. "Nasty".

"Come on, I am busting your chops. I trust you kids. I know you both will do the right thing."

She smooched me on my cheek, leaned over and kissed Veronika. "When we are done eating I got to finish getting ready for my date. Can the both of you put aside your feuding long enough to work together and do the dishes for me, please?"

Sometimes I wish Mom weren't so outspoken and affectionate at times but that is one of the reasons we love her so much.

We did the dishes together. We didn't fight.

Mom's date came by and he looked nice. He was an older blonde guy with slightly graying hair. He could have been Dad's age if Dad hadn't passed away from a heart attack. He was wearing a blue snow jacket. He came into the living room and shook our hands.

"I've a son about your age. Maybe you know him. His name is Jim."

"Jim?"

"Yeah, the kids at school call him 'Big Jim'".

My heart sank. Just great. Mom is dating creepy Big Jim's dad.

"I think I have heard of him."

"Let's go Sinclair." Mom was glowing. I hadn't seen her look this happy in a long time.

"Nice meeting you Billy and Veronika."

Veronika was drooling over him, "Nice meeting you, Mr. Andrews."

"Please call me Sinclair."

"Sinclair."

They left and the door closed.

"You are such a suck-up when it comes to men."

"He is cute and Mom thinks he is cute too."

"Yeah but his son is stink hole number one at school. Maybe he isn't so nice once you get to know him."

"Maybe you are jealous."

"Maybe. Maybe I am right."

I grabbed the book from the table by the door and went upstairs.

I went into my bedroom, turned on the light switch, and plopped down on the bed. I opened the book and before I knew it I was inside the book.

I mean it, I was literally inside the book.

I blinked and all sense of being in a room was gone. I was lying down on what for all intensive purposes was a giant white floor.

It could have been made of linoleum or marble or who knows what.

In front of me was a giant transparent board and on it were the letters "T A B L E O F C O N T E N T S".

"Where am I? What is happening?"

A pleasant sounding male voice said, "Welcome to the Table of Contents. You are inside what you can call "The Burger International Architecture Guide 1947 Edition" or for short, you can call me, Burger."

"Burger? Get me out of here."

"Just to set things straight, Burger was not my real name. I came across this book when somebody dropped it off at a library sale many years ago and I basically copied myself over to look like it. I know I am not quite current with the times but comparatively to where I was at before, this is a lot better."

"Burger! Get me out."

"Billy, you aren't really in anything to get out off."

I blinked and I was back lying on my bed.

"Shhheeeee-hooot." I threw the book down. I rushed into the bathroom and relieved myself. I splashed water on my face. I screamed downstairs. "Veronika?"

"What is it, loser?"

"Nothing."

Okay I wasn't dreaming and I was back in my room. I went back over to my bed. I opened up the book and there was a page that said "Table of Contents" with nothing under it. When I looked up from my bed, I was back in the giant white room.

"You really are just phased slightly out of time and space. You haven't gone anywhere, Billy. Anybody looking at you will think you are deep in thought reading a book and you can leave anytime. Go ahead and try it. Nobody is going to try and stop you."

"Okay." I blinked and I was back in my room.

I looked back at the book, and I was back in the white room. I started to get sick and blinked.

I ran over to the bathroom and started to throw up the turkey. It was like when I first started playing first person shooters on the computer and games consoles. I would get dizzy and sick. After awhile I got use to it. I wondered if I would ever get use to whatever this was.

I went back over to the book, took it into the bathroom with me and opened it. I was back in the white room.

"Okay, what is this?"

"This is the Table of Contents for The Burger International Architecture Guide 1947 Edition. Please call me Burger."

"Burger."

"You are now part of the Library."

"Can I go back to being sick now?"

Mr. Ptolemy

The satellite service man was scratching his head. He had tried thirteen different times to get the satellite web service working and it still would not get a clear signal. "I am sorry, sir. I don't have any idea what is going on. We are getting a clear signal on my meter and you should be connected to the Internet."

I would be to, if some of the Library would let me, Ptolemy thought.

"Well, let's try again next week. For right now, I will pay for the service call and you can leave the connections here at the library with the other ones."

There were plenty of other connections. Two attempts at cable, three at dsl, even old 300 baud modems did not work in the Library. The forces that kept the Library in balance, if that would be the word, also kept the Library from trying to reach out and touch people in a more efficient manner.

It would only be a matter of time, Ptolemy thought. He escorted the serviceman out after signing his service sheet. Ptolemy locked the Library, not that it needed locks. It was only a formality since the Library could defend itself.

He walked over to the reference section, pulled two books out and opened them in front of him. He closed his eyes, assumed a yogic position and began to float in the air.

Ptolemy opened his eyes and he was floating in what looked like a Roman temple. Before him were two books floating as well.

One of them was simply called, "Applied Physics". The other one had an innocent title of, "Application of Eye Liner and Make-Up for Girls! 1969".

"Another failure?" the Physics book asked.

"We appear to be too evenly balanced. We need something to tip the scales in our favor."

The Application of Eye Liner book shimmered and took the form of an attractive raven-haired woman wearing nothing but a toga and flat sandals. "If nothing else, we have patience and time. And no fire nor water can hurt us anymore."

"There is that," the Physics book said. The book shimmered and turned into a middle-aged man with a salt and pepper colored beard. He too was wearing a toga and sandals. "Any progress in trying to get some of the other reference material to our cause?"

"None," Ptolemy said with disgust. "It would be easier to get everybody in the Middle East to forget what their ancestors did and start as brothers and sisters as if nothing happened then to connect to the Internet."

The woman, who was spirit from the Application of Eye Liner and Make-Up for Girls! 1969, walked over to the men. "Make peace in the Middle East? We haven't tried that yet. If that is what it takes, perhaps we should do that. People would rally to our cause if we show them that we can bring peace."

"It would not suit well with the more radical texts that are in the Library," the Physics book/man stated while stroking his chin.

"I am going to try and get the town to take a more proactive approach to helping us."

"How, Ptolemy? And what would you do different this time?" asked the Eye Liner book/woman as she walked over and placed her hands on his shoulders.

"We are having our Readers and Civic Leaders Day in two days. I think we need to take some of the reference books out and see if they can help the community."

The Physics book/man frowned. "Be careful and don't do anything stupid. The balance is pretty delicate as is and we don't want any of the texts to defect to the other side."

"Don't worry. I have things under control."

Ptolemy closed his eyes and when he opened them he was floating back in the Library in front of two open books. He floated to the ground and stretched his legs.

"And when I have things under my absolute control, my dear books," he thought to himself, "we will do things my way."

Billy North

Billy came out of the bathroom after gargling with mouthwash to rinse the smell of puke out. He went back over to the book and picked it up. He was transported back to the white room.

"Okay, so what happens now?"

"What do you want to happen?"

"Where are you?"

"Here". A middle-aged man wearing a toga and sandals appeared in front of him. "It is I, Burger. Actually, I am doing this for your benefit. This is what I use to look like a long time ago. "

"I don't get any of this."

Burger placed a hand on Billy's shoulder. Billy could feel his touch and Burger's hand was warm. Warm burger, he thought.

"You actually are still in your room and your consciousness has been connected to my consciousness through the book because I extended an invitation to you and you accepted it. Remember that feeling about finding an old friend back at the library?"

The feeling came back to Billy and he relaxed. "Yeah, hey you aren't hypnotizing me or trying to abuse me are you?"

Burger frowned. "You are here of your own free will. Some parts of the Library are abusive but the part that I am in respects individuality and free will. I am part of the Library. You can be part of it to, if you want."

"What is the Library?"

"The great Library of Alexandria, considered one of the original eight wonders of the world but it is more than that. It is the keeper of great words of power and creation. I sense that you can help us and be a guardian to protect these gifts or if need be, destroy them."

Burger sat down next to Billy and before him, a great palace from thousands of years ago appeared in front of him. People in togas appeared walking next to him and then through him.

"Wow! Is this a hologram?"

"Something like that, Billy." This is what the Library looked like thousands of years ago. "You are looking at it through my eyes. People came all over the known world to share information and learn from the Library."

The scene changed for Billy as he saw the Library breaking down as if going back in time. "The Library was originally put together where people tried to duplicate the first sounds."

"Wow." Billy watched in awe as he saw men and women turning into swirls of energy and crashing into one another.

"The first sounds of what created this universe. We listened. We prayed. We thought we were able to duplicate the sounds of the universe. We didn't quite get it right. We did get an approximation and that granted human beings incredible powers. Some people grafted themselves through prayer and magic into these sounds. We didn't have means of recording sounds. They turned into books."

"Are any of the books tapes, cds or dvds now? How come you haven't gotten on the internet?"

"We have a checks and balances system for that," Burger laughed. "It would be too easy for one side of the Library to win over the other side if they could actually succeed in recording their sounds on a medium other than books. We also are actively keeping any modern recording devices from recording us."

The images changed and Billy saw people reading scrolls in great rooms lit with oil lamps.

"This is wild".

"People from all over the world came to learn how to improve their lives, their communities and make the world a better place."

The scene changed to gladiators fighting with older sinister-looking men behind the lines of warriors holding books instead of swords and spears. "Unfortunately, men also used the power of the Library to wage battles."

The images faded and Billy found himself in his room. Burger continued, "Okay, we are now in your room, but not in your room. I am projecting an image of your room inside the book and you are inside the book. Notice that your eyes are still closed?"

Billy reacted, "Huh! I didn't even realize it!"
Billy opened his eyes and his room looked
the same except he was holding the book in
his hands. When he closed his eyes, he
was lying on his bed but the book wasn't
there!

"So tight! I see."

"What did you notice?"

"There is no book in this room. That means
I am in the book, right?"

"Bravo!", Burger exclaimed. "You have
figured it out. If you ever need to discern if
you are in a book, or the Library or the real
world, look to see if the actual book is in
your hands. One day, knowing the
difference may save your life. Now, let me
show you about this book."

Billy found himself sitting in the center of a
huge field of grass.   He could smell cut
grass!

"Billy, I am called the International Architecture Guide 1947 Edition. I figured we would start with a clean slate or in this case, an open field and I will let you explore this book. I want you to think of making a house out of grass."

"Like a hut? Like if I was stranded on an island?"

"Sure, that would be great."

Billy imagined that the ground in front of him would change into a grass hut. The grass in front of him started moving and formed a small, green and brown hut about 1 foot tall and 1 foot wide with a brown thatched roof. "I didn't even have to think hard to get it formed! Rocking!"

"Billy, you haven't seen the best of it yet. Open your eyes," Burger requested.

Billy opened his eyes. He looked down and saw the book in his hands. Slowly, he looked around his room. He saw his models, his books and on the floor by his bed was the very same grass hut that he had imagined! He reached down and touched it. It felt wet like it was just watered and it had a smell. It smelled like freshly cut grass.

He heard a voice come from the book, "Here is one of the biggest secrets of the books from the Library. Whatever you think of in the book, will appear in the real world. Be VERY careful what you think of and you need to practice on scale. That means the size of what you are thinking of. Now, I want you to make it go away. Close your eyes and think of it vanishing."

Billy closed his eyes and was back in the book. He thought of the grass hut disappearing. It did. He opened his eyes and it was gone.

"Mom would have killed me if I had grass and dirt here in the room."

He closed his eyes again and thought of an ice cream soda. Nothing appeared. "Hey,

Burger. How come when I think of an ice cream soda, nothing is appearing?"

"That's easy, Billy. I am a book on architecture. I can only help you manifest things that would be in buildings, houses or any kind of dwelling. Try thinking of a picture of an ice cream soda."

Billy concentrated and a framed picture of a chocolate ice cream soda in a glass appeared. He opened his eyes. The picture was sitting in his room as well!

"Okay, I think I get it. Anything that can be considered part of building I can create." Billy paused for a second. He took the book, and left his room.

"I'm going for a walk," Billy yelled at his sister.

"Yeah, whatever, just don't get killed or Mom will blame me," she screamed back.

He threw on a jacket, his shoes and went outside. It was dark. He walked down till he got to the park. The park was empty for now. Nobody was walking their dog and the streetlamps were dim and in need of repair. It would be a great place to experiment.

Billy walked into the center of a baseball diamond. He looked around to make sure there wasn't anybody around. There was very little traffic around the park.

"Let's see what I can do." Billy opened the book and after a split second of disorientation looked down and did not see the book in his hands. Other than that, it looked like he was outside standing in the baseball diamond. "He concentrated on four wooden walls appearing around him and a roof. The walls took shape as did the roof.

He opened his eyes.

Billy was standing inside a small doorless room that he had made in the baseball diamond!

"I guess I better make a door."

He closed his eyes and thought about making a door. On one of the walls, an outline of a door started forming until a dark, wooden door appeared with a silver turn handle. Billy opened his eyes and looked at the door.

"Let's test it." He walked over, opened the door and walked out. The walls collapsed inward. Billy jumped away as the walls and door slammed into the baseball field raising small dirt clouds.

"What?"

The book spoke, "Watch it! You didn't bother to make the walls connect to anything did you? They didn't fall on you because of your force of will but once you walked out of the way, gravity took over. You are going to focus on connecting the walls. Be careful because you don't want to do anything that might get you killed."

"I'll try to remember that, Burger," Billy closed his eyes and wished the room away to start from scratch.

Mabel's Book of Weapons 1976

This one was slow. At least he showed
great potential to be cruel. That made
Mabel happy. Big Jim was walking around
his room. He had all sorts of handguns
and rifles scattered on the floor. There were
Colt 45 handguns, Mausers, sub machine
guns and even Kentucky long rifles. He
had an M-16 in his arms.

"Big Jim, start wishing away some of these
guns. You need to be more focused."

"No. I want to shoot something now."

If Mabel had eyes she would be rolling
them, "Listen, I am letting you make all the
guns you want for practice. Have you
noticed that not one of them has bullets in
them? None of them have firing pins? You
kids today and your video game generation
- you want it all and now," Mabel mockingly
talked in Jim's voice.

Jim scowled. "You have to do what I tell you to. You suck and you have to listen to me. Mr. Ptolemy told me!"

"I do, but only to a point." Mabel materialized a silver small, two-barrel derringer and floated it in front of Jim.

Right between his eyes.

Jim tried to jump back but found he couldn't move. He dropped the M-16.

"Heyy, jerk, what gives?"

"You need to work on focus, Big Jim. Firepower and winning battles isn't about a lot of guns. It is learning how to use one or two and using them wisely. "

The derringer cocked itself.

"I'll listen, okay." Jim tried turning his head away.

The derringer zoomed close to his face. Just as the trigger pulled, there was an excessively bright powder flash. The barrel turned skywards and the small bullet missed Jim, flew up and vanished.

"Arrgh, you shot me, hot. Hot!!!"

"Relax," Mabel laughed, "I just made an extra large powder blast. Half your face will look sooty and sore but you'll live. The next time you give me any heat though, I won't miss."

"Okay, okay, I'm sorry, I'm sorry. I will do one thing at a time! I promise! Owwww."

Mabel had dealt with these types of punks before and it was better they knew who was boss now and started towing the line. With enough practice and discipline, this one might work out.

And if Big Jim didn't work out, she would kill him and have Ptolemy get her another kid.

Billy North

Billy was focusing on making screws and
hinges and materializing them as sides to a
door. That was hard work!

He opened his eyes and tested the door.
He walked out and closed it.

"Good," Burger said. "You are getting it. It
is the details that will make you a master of
the Library. If you concentrate and focus
on the details as well as the big picture you
can do anything."

Billy collapsed and fell to the ground. "I
don't feel like I can do anything. I am dead
tired and I think I better get home before
Mom comes back from her date."

Billy closed his eyes and wished the room
and door away. He wished for a comfy sofa
chair underneath him. He felt himself lift
off the cold grass and opened his eyes. He
was sitting in a big black leather chair.

"Ahhhhh!", Billy exclaimed, as he sank into the chair.

"If you are going to be prepared for battle, you need to be able to materialize everything and anything you can and understand how to use it."

"What do you mean, Burger?"

"If somebody is shooting at you, what would you do?"

"Ah, think of a wall."

"Let's try that."

Billy closed his eyes and saw a three-foot round metal pipe flying at him. He imagined a brick wall in front of him.

The wall appeared, and the pipe slammed into it causing the bricks to buckle.

"That was a good start but what about this?"

Another 3-foot metal pipe came from another side flying and Billy quickly wished for another wall. Upon contact the pipe grew to be twenty feet in diameter plowing through the wall and as Billy cringed he watched the pipe turn into daisies.

As the yellow daisies covered him in his chair, Burger continued, "What would have happened if something had exploded on contact with you? What if it sends pieces of the wall into you? You need to be able to run away, think quickly and 'out of the book', so to speak to come up with different defensive and offensive tactics. Trust me, in combat, there are books in the Library who won't be attacking you with daisies!"

"I don't think I can handle this battle thing."

"You are just tired, Billy. You are a master - you just don't know it yet. Let's clean up and go home and get some sleep and we can continue after school tomorrow. Just remember - don't do things by the book, do

things using the book. Use some
imagination!"

Billy started wishing for the daisies, the
chair and everything to go away. He tried
hard not to imagine what kind of creative
enemies he would be facing and how to stop
them without getting killed.

If It's Yummy, I'm Hungry!

Another phenomenon was happening at the Library.

Hungry was hungry. He felt he had been running in the sand for days. His hair was covered with sand.

Leo and Woofy, two guardians of the Library, had tried burying him under sandstorms several times.

Like that would work.

Hungry patiently dug like a mole through the sand, watching it fall in and through his giant mouth as he dug himself out. He would climb out of the sand, start running and promptly get buried again.

Instinctively he thought they must be getting tired. He stuck out his giant tongue and could taste in the sandy air the direction they were in. He started running towards them.

Leo was a yellow-haired boy in yellow swim trunks with a pail and shovel. Woofy was a small, black Scottish terrier. The dog growled as Hungry got closer.

Leo raised his hands in front of the dog. "Woofy, no! Go tell the others that Hungry is loose. I will slow him down."

The dog whimpered.

"Now! I love you too and it's been fun, just go! Scoot!"

Woofy scampered off.

Hungry didn't care what the dog was up to. Hungry was hungry. He lumbered and then started galloping on all four of his legs towards Leo.

"No, hungry. I won't let you get any further." Leo raised his hands and a blistering sand storm started stinging Hungry. Hungry closed his beady eyes and concentrated and his black hair grew thicker. He opened his mouth as Leo started to run.

In a dark corner of the Library, on a shelf with only two books, the book, "If It's Yummy, I'm Hungry", opened up and grabbed a small children's book called "Leo and Woofy's Day At the Beach." Like a bear trap snapping down steel razor teeth in one bite on animal flesh, the children's book was swallowed whole but not before the Table of Contents page, half torn reading "Woofy's Day At the Beach", sprung out of the snapping book and floated to a spot on the shelf.

Mr. Ptolemy had watched the act of book cannibalism and quietly muttered an obscenity.

Excerpt From Fun Facts of the Ancient World 1102 AD Edition

Fun Fact #5 - The Library is a living thing. Like all living things, things do not work perfectly and cells can misfire, just like in human beings.

Trusted friend, one of the most astonishing things about the Library is that it collectively is a living force on it's own. If you think of the Library like a human body, you will know that different parts can function doing different things. They also can have cells that misfire. In humans that has caused cancer or mutations.

Let us say that over thousands of years, some of the energy from the Library in a book that has accumulated but never been used by a human started to misfire and grow not unlike like a cancer or as doctors would say, a teratoma.

What is a teratoma? A teratoma is generally thought to be a benign quasi-embryonic cell that has gone wrong. Think of it as a tumor involving an egg. So in the case of Hungry, think of Hungry as an unfertilized concentrated book that over thousands of years started growing wild. And in this case, it grew by feeding on the energy of other books. All it ever did or knows how to do is eat.

In ancient times, Hungry was considered a Titan, one of the primal forces of the universe. It was energy that just kept growing. The Library has joined together over the years at times to diminish and control Hungry. It is too wild and cannot be destroyed or at least we have not found a way yet without destroying the entire Library.

In your Modern Era, Hungry took over a children's book, "If It's Yummy, I'm Hungry". It has, until recently, been kept under lockdown by various books in the Library.

Fun Fact #6 - It is Up to the Head Librarian To Keep Hungry and any other Titans From Getting Loose.

Whatever agenda the Head Librarian has, he needs to put aside whatever he is doing and work to insure that the Titans never get loose.

Ever.

Billy North

Billy had practiced for two hours that night. He was exhausted. Mom had come back from her date ecstatic.

"That is one of the nicest guys I have ever met," she said to Billy and Veronika.

Billy had returned the signed consent form to the Library the next day. Mr. Ptolemy was staring at him like he was some piece of dirt.

Over the next two days, Billy quietly snuck out and practiced again and again.

School went by uneventfully. Billy didn't see much of Tricia, except for class. He wanted to spend more time with her but he felt a definite urgency in getting up to speed in using his book.

Finally, it was Readers and Civic Leaders Day.

Tricia and he had walked over to the library after school.

The Library was filled with kids. Other than Mr. Ptolemy, there weren't any adults around.

Everybody there was holding onto a book.

Mr. Ptolemy looked at the students with a smirk on his face. "Today is Readers and Civic Leaders Day, boys and girls. This is the day that we plan on writing papers about doing good things for the community – like trying to improve Internet access –"

The children exploded in cheers.

"And trying to get more involved with the workings of the community! I want each of you to -"

"Hey, jerk. Come here."

Billy turned around and felt the smack of a Colt .45 revolver gun butt against the side

of his head. He started crying and began to
catch himself.

It was Big Jim. He was carrying Mabel's
Book of Weapons 1976 in one hand.   In
the other hand he held a revolver towards
Billy's head. He then brought his hand
down. Jim started spinning his revolver
like an old time cowboy Billy had seen in
the movies.

He closed his eyes to connect with Burger.

"This kid is nuts," Burger said.

Billy could hear Mr. Ptolemy screaming at
Big Jim but couldn't make out the words.

It sounded like "No guns allowed in the
Library!".

"Time to take this outside." Billy
concentrated on the building pipes from the
Library coming up like metal tentacles and
pushing Big Jim backwards at jet speed.

Big Jim didn't know what hit him. He dropped his revolver as he flew violently out the front of the Library doors.

Billy and the other students ran after him. The students were yelling and screaming.

"Fight! Fight!"

"Teach that bully a lesson!"

As Billy raced outside he heard what sounded like guns cocking. He quickly wished up brick walls around him as he heard the pinging and budda-budda sounds of machine gun fire.

"I gotta keep moving. He has been practicing too."

Billy formed a long large tunnel aiming for the woods behind the Library. He wished for a giant plush chair with wheels. Billy was rolling down the tunnel faster and faster.

Behind him, he could hear explosions. Big Jim had gotten into the tunnel. He heard gunfire. Bullets whizzed by above him.

He came to the end of the tunnel in the woods behind the town. He got out and started concentrating.

An armored car came roaring out of the tunnel. On top of the armored car, a machine gun was firing next to a loudspeaker.

"You are soo dead," Jim boomed from the loudspeaker.

"No, you are!" Billy yelled.

As the armored car came out of the tunnel a church steeple rose out of the ground and pierced through the undercarriage of the vehicle.

The armored car was lifted into the air twenty feet. Other church steeples started jutting out of the earth piercing the car like magician's swords slamming through a magic box.

The difference was instead of a pretty assistant Big Jim was sitting inside. He started screaming like a little girl.

"Owwww, owww, you are crushing the car into me. I can't breathe!"

Billy wished for the steeples to recede back into the ground. He walked over to the crumpled mass that was the armored car. The car started vanishing and Big Jim was lying on the ground gasping and his book was next to him.

Billy could hear Big Jim's book.

"You are a waste. And now I am going to waste you."

A revolver appeared in mid air by Big Jim's head.

Billy screamed, "No!"

He concentrated and a brick wall rose up brushing against Jim. Bullets smashed into the brick wall and stayed there.

"Get control of your book, Jim. Come on, you are in charge, not the book."

"I, I'm scared."

"It's okay to be scared, just don't let it make you do things that you don't want to do."

"I-I'll try-y," he stammered.

Big Jim slowly got to his feet. His book floated into the air, tried spinning around and fell flat at Jim's feet.

"See! You did it!"

Jim smiled as the revolver and the brick wall vanished.

Mabel grumbled, "I hate children."

"Too bad, you gotta listen to me. I-I did it. Hey, Billy, I am sorry man. You know, you are all right by me, man. I was wrong to point a gun at you."

Billy smiled. "Thanks, man."

"Gentlemen," Burger interrupted, "We need to get back to the library. Something horrible is happening there."

"I'll drive this time, Jim."

Billy materialized a sofa with wheels. Jim picked up his book. Both Jim and he sat down on it.

"Let's go!" Billy concentrated and the sofa started zooming back towards the Library.

If It's Yummy, I'm Hungry!

Hungry had grown. The commotion in the Library had attracted his attention and the giant creature lumbered through the rotunda. Children were grabbing their books and trying things to stop him.

One boy opened his book, "Music Music", and the sound of a thousand orchestras blasted into Hungry.

The windows on the Library shattered. Children covered their ears and started crying.

Hungry winced, lunged forward and swallowed the boy and his book in one bite.

Children were fleeing the Library. Bookcases had fallen. Veronika was crying. Her leg was caught under a thick wooden bookcase. Tricia was trying to move the case.

Mr. Ptolemy crawled over with a book under his arm. He opened the book, "Ants and Plants", and thousands of ants came crawling out. They marched at lightning speed under the case and effortlessly up righted it.

"Quickly, get out of here. I will stall the thing."

Mr. Ptolemy closed his eyes and dozens of palm, bamboo and eucalyptus trees shot up out of the floorboards of the Library and caged Hungry.

Hungry roared.

"That won't hold him for long," Mr. Ptolemy said as he opened his eyes.

Tricia supported Veronika as she grabbed her book and started walking towards the front door.

Billy and Big Jim rolled up in their sofa. They climbed off of it as they entered the

Library. They couldn't believe what they were seeing.

Billy looked at Veronika. He looked at her leg. "Are you hurt, Veronika?"

"I think it might be broken but for now I will live."

Mr. Ptolemy ran out to the children. "Change of plans. I need you – ALL of you- to try and help me stop Hungry."

"Hungry?" Big Jim questioned. "Was that from a food book or something?"

"Something like that," Ptolemy said as he waved his hand dismissively, "we don't have time for explanations. I need the four of you to try and keep it contained within the trees that I grew."

He produced a small book out of his pocket, "I need to read this quickly. You need to buy me some time."

Hungry roared.

"Okay, okay," Billy said. "Let's do this. Veronika, can you move?"

"Not without screaming. Can you and Big Jim get me close to that thing?"

They nodded. Each boy grabbed an arm and carried Veronika closer to Hungry.

Hungry was thrashing at the trees and leaves. Pieces of wood were flying throughout the Library.

Hungry smelled Veronika's pain and lunged a huge black paw toward's her.

"Stop," Tricia screamed.

Hungry's arm just froze inches away from the children.

"How did you do that?" Billy asked.

She raised her book, "I Love Verbs". "Verbs are pretty powerful commands when you know how to use them, Billy."

Billy and Jim gently lowered Veronika down on the ground. It was covered with leaves and broken branches.

Big Jim concentrated and a harpoon gun appeared in his hands. He fired it and a giant net came from behind the harpoon. It started covering the wood and trees.

The trees started breaking. Hungry was starting to move and tear the net.

"He's breaking free," Tricia said.

Billy concentrated and giant stone pillars came out of the ground and surrounded Hungry.

The stones started to crack.

Mr. Ptolemy came running back with his book. The title of it was "Miniaturization and Micro Engineering."

He closed his eyes and opened them.

Hungry was starting to shrink. But not fast enough as he started breaking free of his stone prison.

Veronika had a small book in her back pocket. She pulled it out and the building began to shake.

"We've got to get out of here and NOW!"

Mr. Ptolemy agreed. "Yes, now!"

"I don't get it," Big Jim said.

"My book is 'California Disasters' and there is nothing more disastrous than an earthquake!"

The boys and Tricia helped Veronika get out of the Library. Mr. Ptolemy was behind them. He was watching as they escaped to make sure that Hungry continued to shrink.

Once outside, they placed Veronika off to the side safely.

Mr. Ptolemy stroked his chin. "Should be okay to go back inside now."

"Are you nuts?" Billy asked.

Mr. Ptolemy smirked. "My dear boy, one of the fun facts about the Library is that it can't be destroyed by earth anymore. An earthquake is just an annoyance."

Big Jim stayed with Veronika as Tricia and Billy joined Mr. Ptolemy.

They walked back inside.

Everything looked normal. There were no signs of any kind of a struggle. The glass on the windows was restored. The books were back in their places.

The only exception was a small stone book on the floor.

"Well, I better get those books and children that Hungry swallowed out of there," Mr. Ptolemy said as he picked up the stone book that imprisoned Hungry.

EPILOGUE

The Readers and Civic Leaders Day was postponed indefinitely.

Billy's mom continued to date Big Jim's dad. That turned out to be great for Billy because he and Big Jim became fast friends. They would practice with their books together creating things.

Veronika's leg healed and Tricia started coming over to the house more often.

As for the Library and Mr. Ptolemy?

Did the Library ever get a good internet connection?

What about the other books?

Those are tales for another time. There are more books and stories just waiting to be told about the Inappropriate Library....

Author's Gratitude

Thank you for buying this book! I hope you enjoyed the first of what should be many adventures with the Inappropriate Library.

Part of the proceeds from sales from this book go to Rett Syndrome research. By buying this book you are helping find a cure for Rett Syndrome. A girl is born with Rett Syndrome every five hours. Boys born with the Rett gene generally die at birth.

Kim Greenblatt

www.ingramcontent.com/pod-product-compliance
Lightning Source LLC
Chambersburg PA
CBHW050833180626
46814CB00004B/1597